W9-AJP-381

Cataloging-in-Publication Data has been applied for and may be obtained from the Library of Congress.

ISBN: 978-1-4197-0787-2

First published in hardcover in Great Britain by HarperCollins Children's Books in 2013. HarperCollins Children's Books is a division of HarperCollins Publishers Ltd.

Printed and bound in China
10 9 8 7 6 5 4 3 2 1

Abrams Books for Young Readers are available at special discounts when purchased in quantity for premiums and promotions as well as fundraising or educational use. Special editions can also be created to specification. For details, contact specialsales@abramsbooks.com or the address below.

ABRAMS
THE ART OF BOOKS SINCE 1949
115 West 18th Street
New York, NY 10011
www.abramsbooks.com

For Armin and
Mexican cyclists

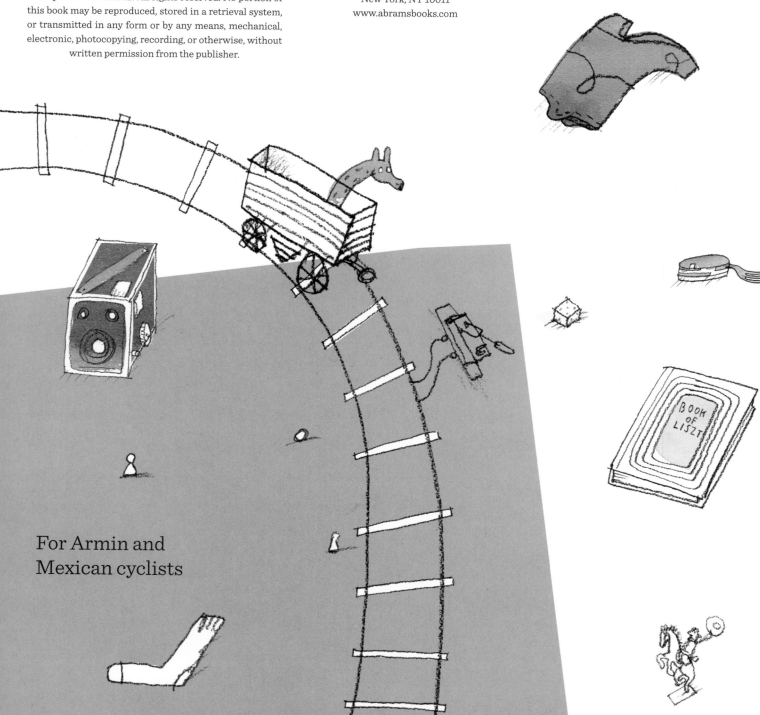

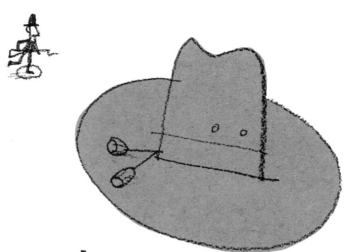

STANDING IN for LINCOLN GREEN

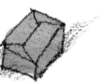

David Mackintosh

Abrams Books for Young Readers

New York

Lincoln Green has a double.
Someone who looks just like him.
A match. SNAP!

His own mother can't tell the
difference between him and
You Know Who.

Having a double gives
Lincoln Green more time to
do only the things he wants
to do . . .

"Woo-
hoo!"

Because the other things that MUST BE DONE TODAY, like tidying and putting away, straightening up and sorting out, will still be done just fine by his handy stand-in . . .

You Know Who.

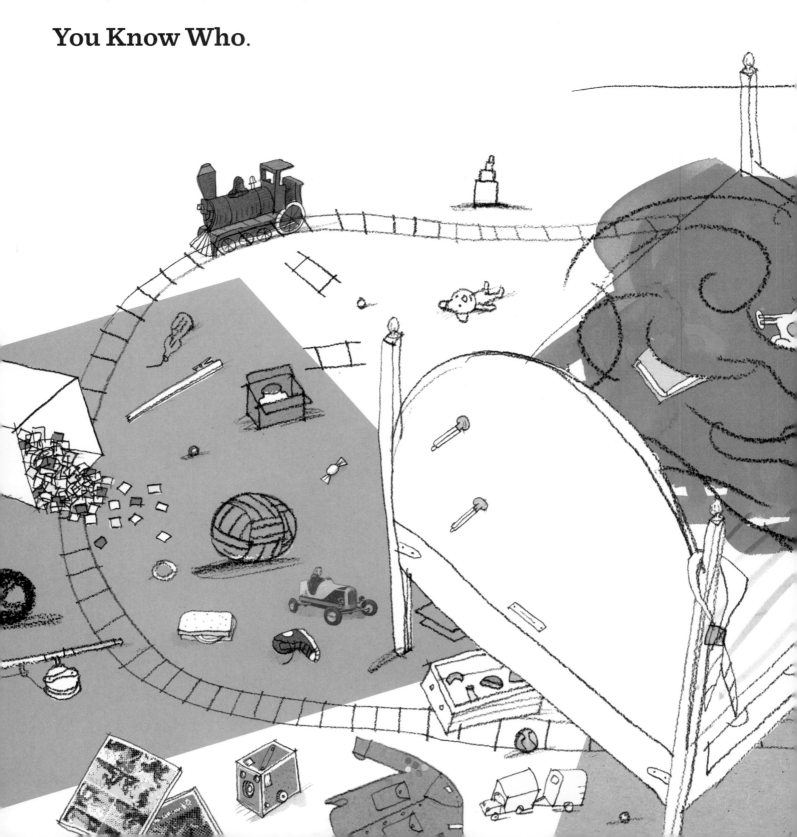

Lincoln Green can grab some shuteye, listen to *Sagebrush and Dawgies* on the radio, and mosey over to Brian and Kenny's place to shoot the breeze. There's plenty of time for fizzy sarsaparilla and hot dogs too.

While things that JUST CAN'T WAIT to be practiced, picked up, polished and cleaned, moved and hung back up, combed, brushed, folded and buttoned are all done just fine, just the same, by You Know Who.

Soon, though,
EVERYTHING
Lincoln Green doesn't
fancy doing himself is on
a list of things-to-do for
You Know Who.

Watering the plants, homework, and returning the Field Trip Permission Slip are all on the list.

Lincoln Green makes the most of every opportunity for You Know Who to help out.

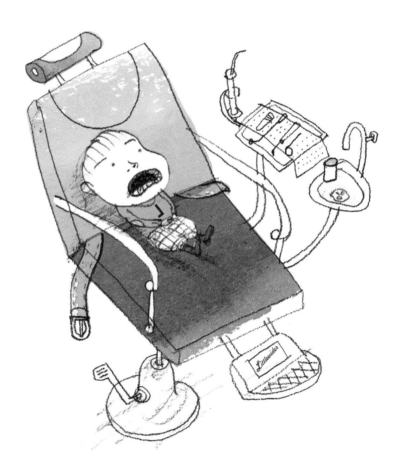

But one day, when You Know Who is painting the fence because it JUST HAS TO BE DONE TODAY and CANNOT WAIT . . .

"Hello, I'm Billy. Who are you?"

"I'm standing in for Lincoln Green."

"What for?"

"He's got better things to do, I suppose."

"Like what?" asks Billy.

"Like timing handstands in his bedroom."

"Oh," says Billy. "Why don't you come over and help me make a tree house? I have two hammers, rope, and an awl. You can paint a fence any old time."

Making a tree house with Billy the kid next door sounds like more fun than whitewashing a whole fence for Lincoln Green.

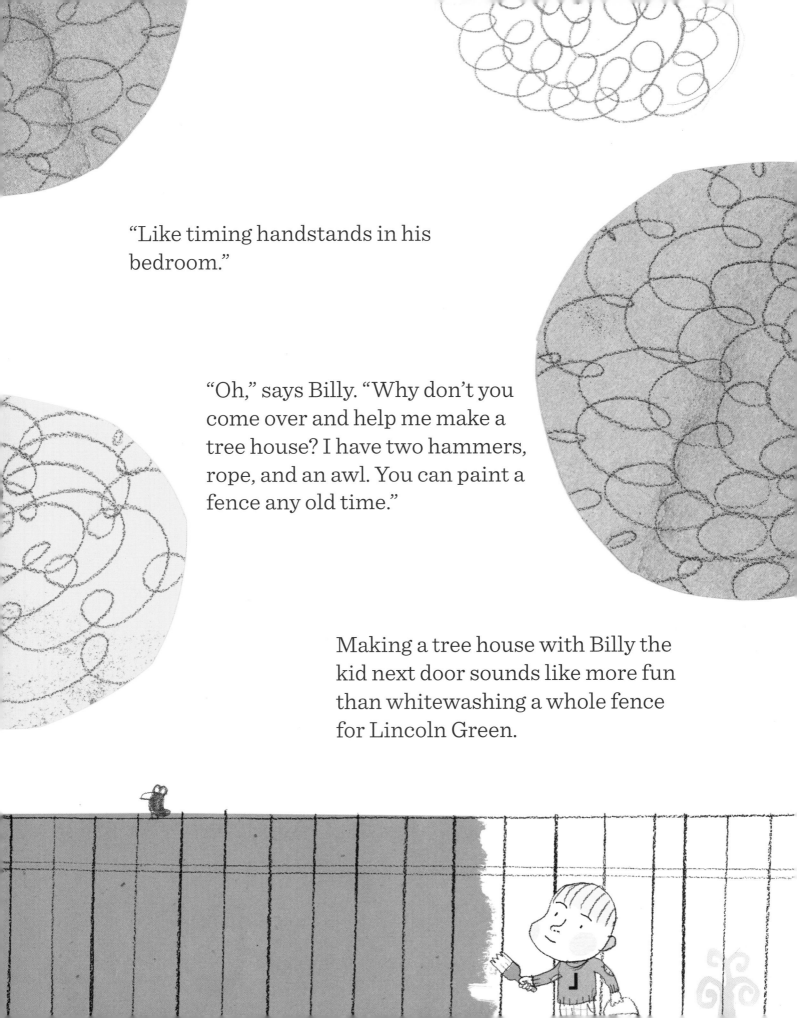

And it is,
that's for sure.

They name it
THE SKY-HIGH
ANYTHING CLUB,
because they can do
anything they like there.

And it is strictly
MEMBERS ONLY.

They even paint the inside
a cheery white color.

Wednesday is Beans Night,
Thursday is Sarsaparilla Day,
Friday is the Grand Elk Breakfast,
and, well, that's plenty to be getting
on with.

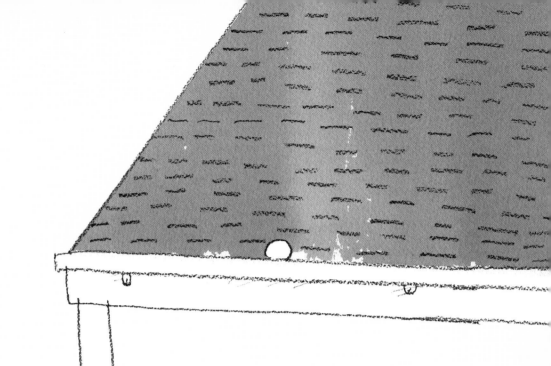

But before
long, there is
big trouble.

It seems Lincoln Green has done nothing his mom has asked.

AND IT'S ALL BECAUSE OF YOU KNOW WHO.

"You're making me look bad," grumbles Lincoln Green. "I'm busy with handstands, swimming, and field trips, so I can't be keeping an eye on you all day."

You Know Who just makes a phizzing noise with his straw.

But Lincoln Green isn't going on
the Field Trip, because he didn't
turn in the Permission Slip.

That night, Kenny calls to tell Lincoln Green about the Field Trip. They saw a snake and a bear eating a fish and Brian accidentally pulled the emergency cord and was spoken to by the conductor.

Lincoln Green would like to have seen that.

What's more . . .

his homework has red Xs on it, because his teacher doesn't give check marks for back-to-front writing.

LINCOLN GREEN HAS HAD ENOUGH!

The next morning,
instead of building the World's Tallest
Tower in his bedroom, Lincoln Green
decides to rake the leaves. HIMSELF.

Every single one.

That's when Billy has a good idea . . .

In no time at all, the boys have rustled up the leaves in a neat pile in the corner of the yard.

"Woo-hoo…"
"Yip-yarr…"
"*Get along thar…*"

"Thanks, neighbor!"
shouts Lincoln Green.

Then Billy swears him into THE HIGH-ALTITUDE HOT FRIES AND KETCHUP CLUB (No Vinegar Allowed).

Lincoln Green says he's going to try to do things himself more often. It's more fun, that's for sure.

Oh, and Lincoln Green's mother is so pleased with him, she gives him a big kiss on the cheek . . .